STAR WARS™

STAR DESTROYER

STAR WARS

STAR DESTROYER

INSIDE THE EMPIRE'S FEARSOME BATTLESHIP

WRITTEN BY
COLE HORTON

INCREDI BUILDS
San Rafael, California

INTRODUCTION

Empires are forged with unstoppable military might. Throughout much of galactic history, that might has been embodied by the Star Destroyer. Part battleship, part command vessel, and part carrier, the Star Destroyer's wedge-shaped hull is an enduring symbol of the Galactic Empire's unquestionable naval power.

Despite its ties to the Galactic Civil War, the Star Destroyer's roots lie not with the Empire, but with the Republic and its Jedi Knights. Shortly after the start of the Clone Wars, *Venator*-class Star Destroyers served the Jedi, delivering their armies of clone troopers to the battlefield to engage the droid navy of the Confederacy of Independent Systems. When Chancellor Palpatine founded the Empire in place of the Republic, Star Destroyers became the backbone of his Imperial Navy. The massive capital ships were produced by the thousands, allowing the Galactic Empire to spread its influence outside of the Core Worlds to the galaxy's distant Outer Rim.

During the Galactic Civil War, Imperial officers would often boast that the sight of just one Star Destroyer in orbit was enough to bring an entire planet under the Empire's control. The craft's fleets of TIE fighters, legions of stormtrooper ground troops and pools of armoured vehicles could be mobilised to lay siege to a planet and quell almost any resistance.

Star Destroyers have played a pivotal role in some of the most crucial galactic conflicts. They defended Coruscant in the final days of the Clone Wars from an attack by General Grievous. At the Battle of Hoth, these capital ships laid siege to the Rebel Alliance's hidden base, forcing the rebels to scatter across the galaxy. At the Battle of Endor, Star Destroyers caught the rebels off guard with a surprise counterattack. During the Battle of Jakku, many brave Star Destroyer captains went down with their ships as the Empire was finally defeated. Despite the loss, remnants of the Empire fled to the farthest regions of space to rebuild in secret.

Rising from the ashes of the Empire decades later, the First Order took the legacy of the Star Destroyer even further. Equipped with the latest in military technology, their Battlecruisers and Dreadnoughts are larger and more powerful than those used by the Empire, ensuring that the Star Destroyer will continue to unleash terror upon the galaxy for years to come.

VENATOR-CLASS STAR DESTROYER

The origins of the Imperial Star Destroyer lie in this Republic-era ship. Though smaller than the ships that followed, Kuat Drive Yard's *Venator*-class served valiantly in hundreds of battles during the Clone Wars, despite often being outnumbered by mass-produced droid ships of the Confederacy of Independent Systems.

CARRIER ROLE

The *Venator*-class was unique among Star Destroyers because of its long dorsal flight deck that ran along the bow of the ship. While it gave the craft the ability to launch wings of starfighters quickly, the flight deck also left the ship vulnerable to boarding and attack while the doors were open.

FORCEFUL COMMAND

During the Clone Wars, the Jedi often used Star Destroyers as their personal flagships, employing them to carry clone trooper battalions to far-flung battlefields or break through Separatist planetary blockades. Jedi Anakin Skywalker's flagship was the *Resolute*, while Obi-Wan Kenobi commanded the *Negotiator*.

CLONE CREW

Most of the crew serving on *Venator*-class ships were genetically identical clones, created in the cloning facilities on Kamino. But when the Republic fell, the clones were phased out in favour of enlisted recruits from Imperial planets across the galaxy.

TECHNICAL SPECIFICATIONS

MANUFACTURER: Kuat Drive Yards

MODEL: *Venator*-class Star Destroyer

LENGTH: 1,137 m

WEAPONRY: 8 heavy turbolaser turrets, 2 medium dual turbolaser cannons, 52 point-defense laser cannons, 4 proton torpedo tubes, 6 tractor beam projectors

HYPERDRIVE: Class 1.0

CREW: 7,400

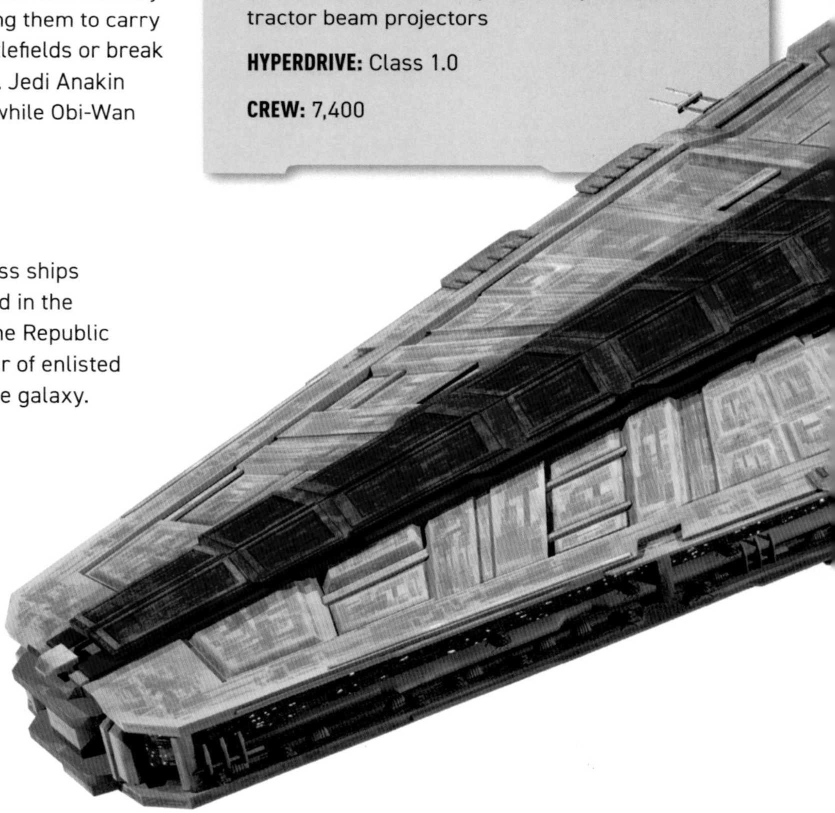

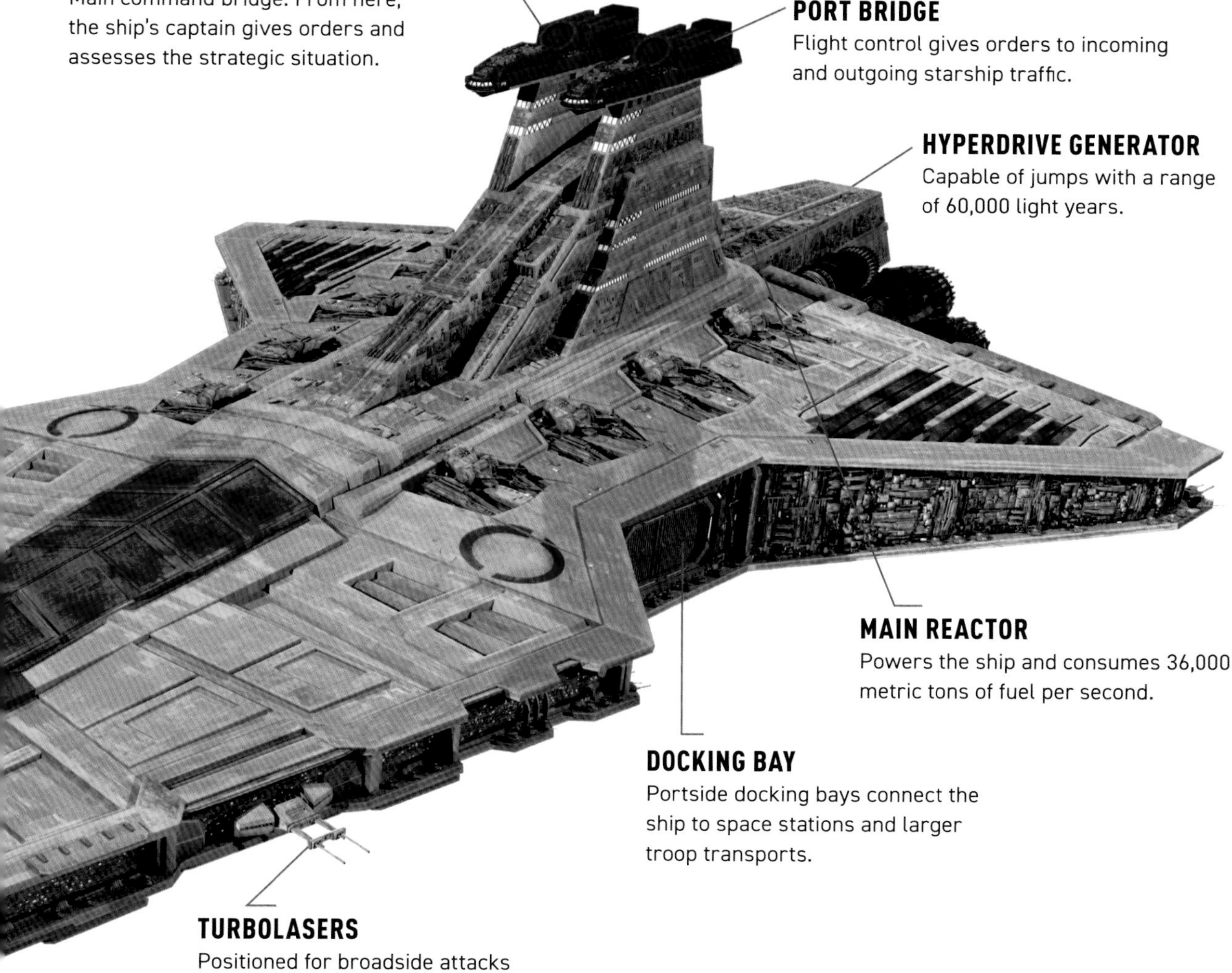

STARBOARD BRIDGE
Main command bridge. From here, the ship's captain gives orders and assesses the strategic situation.

PORT BRIDGE
Flight control gives orders to incoming and outgoing starship traffic.

HYPERDRIVE GENERATOR
Capable of jumps with a range of 60,000 light years.

MAIN REACTOR
Powers the ship and consumes 36,000 metric tons of fuel per second.

DOCKING BAY
Portside docking bays connect the ship to space stations and larger troop transports.

TURBOLASERS
Positioned for broadside attacks against other capital ships.

ESCORT DUTY

When the Clone Wars began at the Battle of Geonosis, the Republic relied on Acclamator-class assault ships to deliver troops, armour, and supplies to the battlefield. The *Acclamator*-class was primarily a transport, more suited for hauling cargo than engaging in combat. The more versatile *Venator*-class would be introduced later in the war.

IMPERIAL STAR DESTROYER

The most common Star Destroyer model was built by the Galactic Empire. Thousands of these ships patrolled the galaxy at the height of the Empire's power and were key to maintaining order, both by intimidation and by force.

TECHNICAL SPECIFICATIONS

MANUFACTURER: Kuat Drive Yards

MODEL: *Imperial I*–class Star Destroyer

LENGTH: 1,600 m

WEAPONRY: 60 Taim & Bak XX-9 heavy turbolaser batteries, 60 Borstel NK-7 ion cannons, 2 dual heavy ion cannon turrets, 2 quad heavy turbolasers, 3 triple medium turbolasers, 2 medium turbolasers, 10 Phylon Q7 tractor beam projectors

HYPERDRIVE: Class 2.0

COMPLEMENT: 72 TIE fighters, 20 AT-AT walkers, 30 AT-ST walkers or AT-DP walkers, 8 *Lambda*-class Imperial shuttles, 15 troop transports

CREW: 9,235 officers, 27,850 enlisted personnel, 9,700 stormtroopers

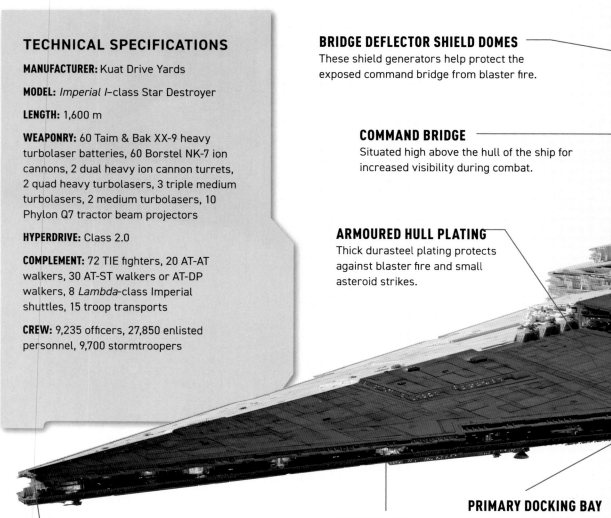

BRIDGE DEFLECTOR SHIELD DOMES
These shield generators help protect the exposed command bridge from blaster fire.

COMMAND BRIDGE
Situated high above the hull of the ship for increased visibility during combat.

ARMOURED HULL PLATING
Thick durasteel plating protects against blaster fire and small asteroid strikes.

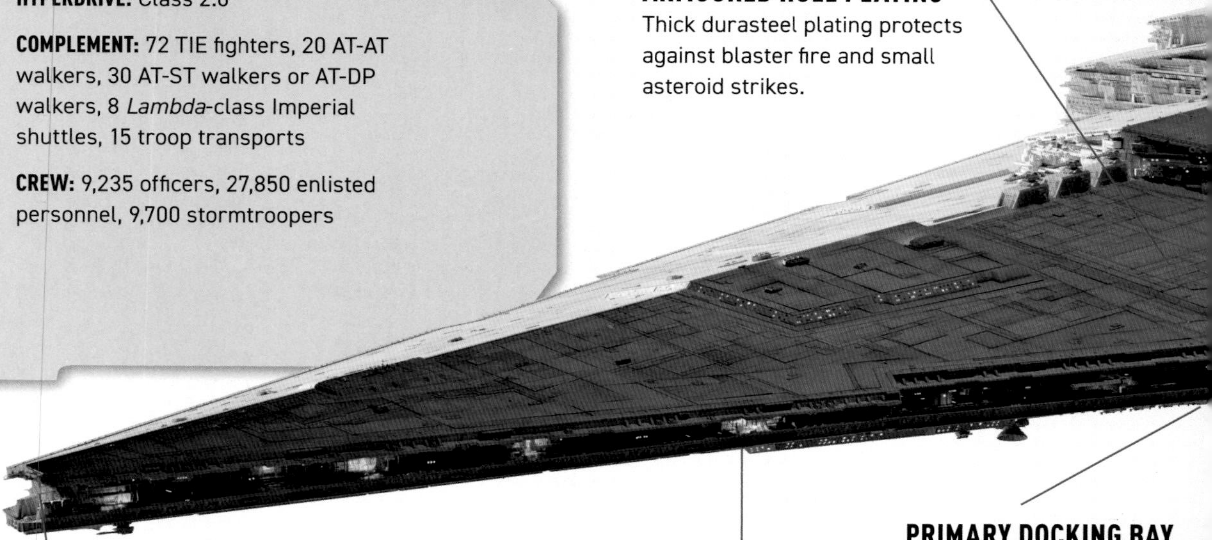

FORWARD TRACTOR BEAM ARRAY
Primarily used to capture other ships in pursuit scenarios.

SECONDARY DOCKING BAY
Typically used to launch smaller ships like TIE fighters.

PRIMARY DOCKING BAY
The largest of two docking ba
Houses shuttles, ground vehic
and fighters.

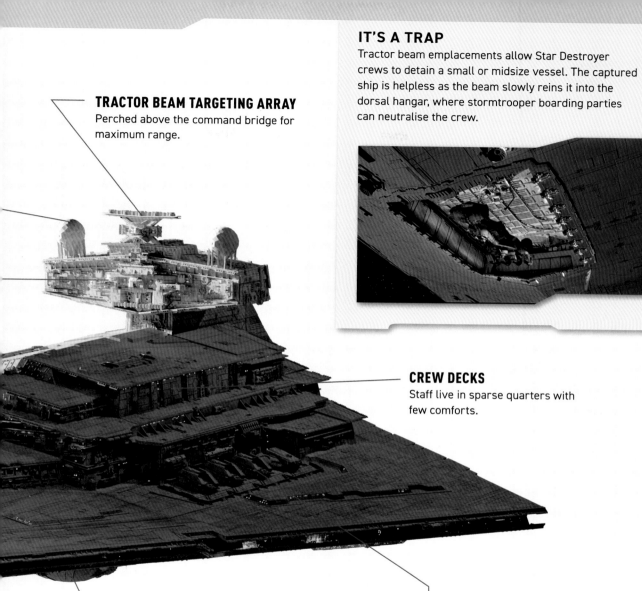

TRACTOR BEAM TARGETING ARRAY
Perched above the command bridge for maximum range.

IT'S A TRAP
Tractor beam emplacements allow Star Destroyer crews to detain a small or midsize vessel. The captured ship is helpless as the beam slowly reins it into the dorsal hangar, where stormtrooper boarding parties can neutralise the crew.

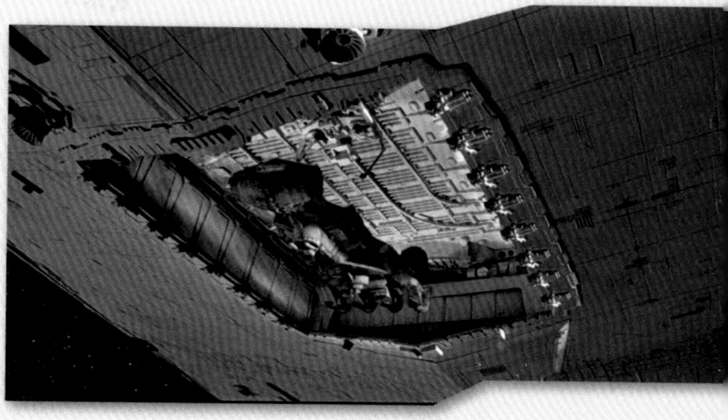

CREW DECKS
Staff live in sparse quarters with few comforts.

MAIN REACTOR
Powers engines, blasters, deflector shields and hyperdrive.

HEAVY TURBOLASER BATTERY
The ship's most deadly weapons, these powerful lasers have a wide range of movement that allows the crew to accurately track targets.

IMPERIAL OFFICERS

Command of a Star Destroyer was one of the most sought-after roles in the Imperial Navy. Many captains worked their entire careers in hopes of taking the helm, yearning for the sense of power and pride that comes from directing such a formidable ship.

EMPIRE'S ELITE

Imperial officers train at academies like those located on Arkanis and Coruscant. While low-performing students join the ranks of the stormtrooper corps, the best become TIE pilots. The TIE pilots who survive the dangers of space combat – and outwit and outscheme their peers – can rise through the ranks to become Star Destroyer captains.

SUPPORT STAFF

It takes thousands of enlisted crew to run a Star Destroyer at peak efficiency. Techs continually monitor the ship's systems, gun crew identify targets and operate weapons systems, and communications crew observe incoming transmissions and decrypt secret Imperial codes.

DANGEROUS TRADE

Star Destroyer officers knew that while it was a great honour to serve at the command of Darth Vader, it was also highly dangerous. During the search for Luke Skywalker and his rebel allies, Captain Needa of the *Avenger* and Admiral Ozzel of the *Executor* both fell victim to the Dark Lord of the Sith's Force-choke, learning the hard way that Vader had little patience for failure.

BATTLEFIELD PROMOTION

After Admiral Ozzel made his last mistake, Darth Vader instantly promoted Firmus Piett to the rank of Admiral and gave him command of the Super Star Destroyer (SSD) *Executor*. Loyal to the Empire and a capable officer, Piett managed to survive his service to Vader until the *Executor* was destroyed during the Battle of Endor.

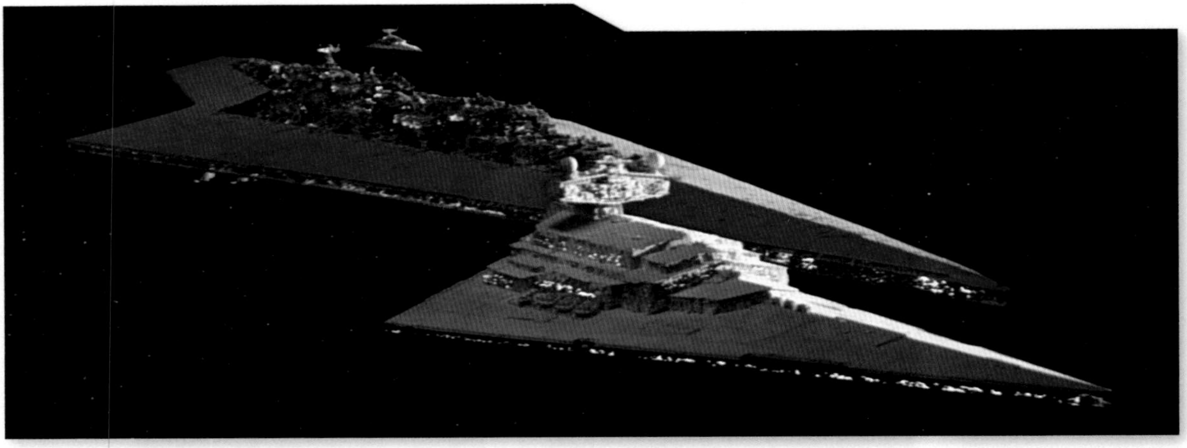

SUPER STAR DESTROYERS

Imperial Dreadnoughts, often known as Super Star Destroyers, were the pinnacle of Imperial Star Destroyer technology. Shrouded in mystery, this model's detailed capabilities and specifications were known only to the most senior Imperial leaders.

TECHNICAL SPECIFICATIONS

MANUFACTURER: Kuat Drive Yards

MODEL: *Executor*-class Star Dreadnought

CLASS: Super Star Destroyer

LENGTH: 19,000 m

WEAPONRY: Thousands of weapons including turbolasers, concussion missile tubes and ion cannons

PROPULSION: 13 engine thrusters

RARE INDEED

Though some suspect the records are incomplete, the Imperial archives suggest that only thirteen Imperial Dreadnoughts existed at the height of the Empire's power. Because of their rarity and extreme cost to produce, they were only given to the Empire's most prominent leaders. The Emperor commanded the *Eclipse*, and Darth Vader's flagship was the *Executor*.

The rest were reserved for high-ranking leaders like Grand General Tagge, who believed that the Empire should have built more Star Destroyers rather than sinking its resources into the moon-sized Death Star.

THE *EXECUTOR*'S END

Under the command of Admiral Piett, the Super Star Destroyer *Executor* was the lead Imperial starship at the Battle of Endor. During the fight, rebel leader Admiral Ackbar ordered a focused attack on the destroyer, urging nimble rebel starfighters to target the *Executor*'s bridge deflector shields. Once the shields were down, a stricken A-wing starfighter collided with the *Executor*'s bridge, killing the command crew, including Piett. Having lost control, the giant capital ship crashed into the space station's surface.

GRAVEYARD AT JAKKU

During the Battle of Jakku, one of the last great battles of the Galactic Civil War, the SSD *Ravager* received critical damage and crashed upside down into the planet's sands. It rests in a region that has become known to locals as the Graveyard of Giants and is picked over by scavengers.

RESURGENT-CLASS BATTLECRUISER

Inspired by the Imperial Star Destroyer's legacy, the First Order has constructed its own massive capital ships that it uses to enforce its iron will on the galaxy.

TECHNICAL SPECIFICATIONS

MANUFACTURER: Kuat-Entralla Engineering

MODEL: *Resurgent*-class Battlecruiser

CLASS: Battlecruiser

LENGTH: 2,915.81 m

WEAPONRY: Point-defense turrets and missile emplacements, tractor-beam projectors, more than 1,500 turbolasers and ion cannons.

CREW: 19,000 officers, 55,000 enlisted personnel, and over 8,000 stormtroopers

THE *FINALIZER*

During his quest to locate Luke Skywalker, Kylo Ren staged several attacks on the Resistance from his personal flagship, the *Finalizer*. Among the decks lie Ren's personal quarters – a sanctuary for brooding meditation – and an interrogation room that he uses when trying to infiltrate the minds of his captives.

HEAVY TURBOLASER BATTERIES
Even more powerful than its predecessors.
FLIGHT DECK
The launching point for First Order TIE spacecraft, shuttles, and troop transports.
TRACTOR BEAM GENERATORS
To snare unsuspecting vessels.

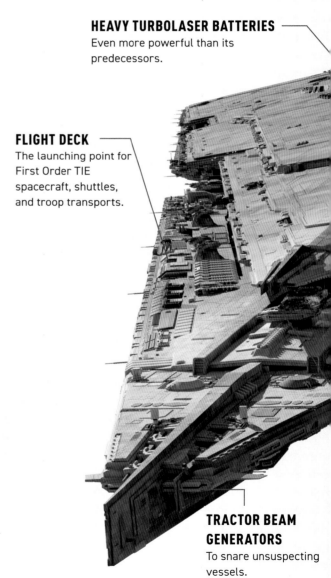

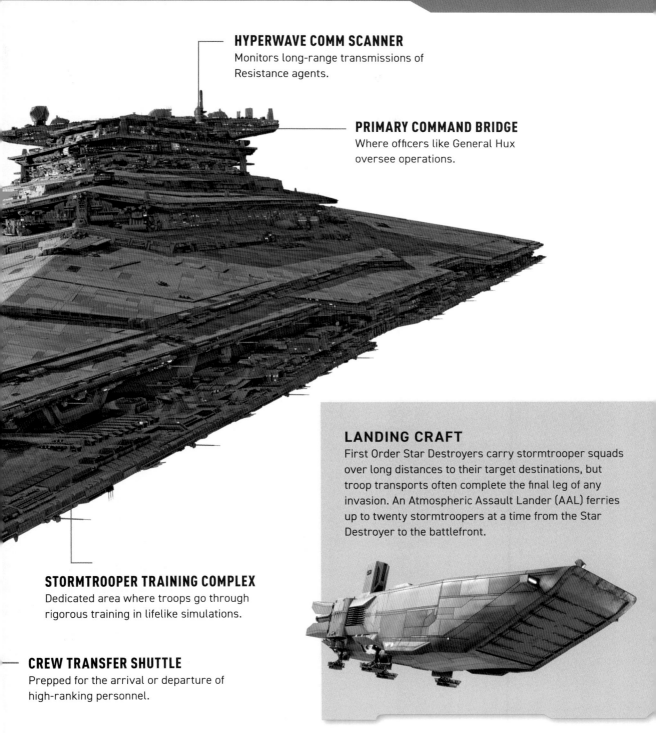

HYPERWAVE COMM SCANNER
Monitors long-range transmissions of Resistance agents.

PRIMARY COMMAND BRIDGE
Where officers like General Hux oversee operations.

STORMTROOPER TRAINING COMPLEX
Dedicated area where troops go through rigorous training in lifelike simulations.

CREW TRANSFER SHUTTLE
Prepped for the arrival or departure of high-ranking personnel.

LANDING CRAFT
First Order Star Destroyers carry stormtrooper squads over long distances to their target destinations, but troop transports often complete the final leg of any invasion. An Atmospheric Assault Lander (AAL) ferries up to twenty stormtroopers at a time from the Star Destroyer to the battlefront.

THE *FULMINATRIX*

One of the First Order's most foreboding craft, this Siege Dreadnought was best known for its powerful bombardment cannons. Resistance Commander Poe Dameron led an attack that destroyed the *Fulminatrix*, but the victory came at a heavy cost for the fighters and bombers under his command.

TECHNICAL SPECIFICATIONS

MANUFACTURER: Kuat-Entralla Engineering

MODEL: *Mandator IV*–class Siege Dreadnought

CLASS: Star Dreadnought

LENGTH: 7,669.71 m

WEAPONRY: 2 orbital bombardment cannons, 26 dorsal point-defense turrets, 6 tractor beam projectors

CREW: 53,000 officers, 140,000 enlisted personnel, and over 22,000 stormtroopers

SHIP TO SHIP

A Siege Dreadnought has ample defenses to protect it from bomber attack, including twenty-six individual point-defense turrets, each manned by a gunner crew, located on the dorsal surface of the ship. The turrets of this ship class are not agile enough to track fast-moving starfighters, however, so the *Fulminatrix* relied on TIE fighters for protection.

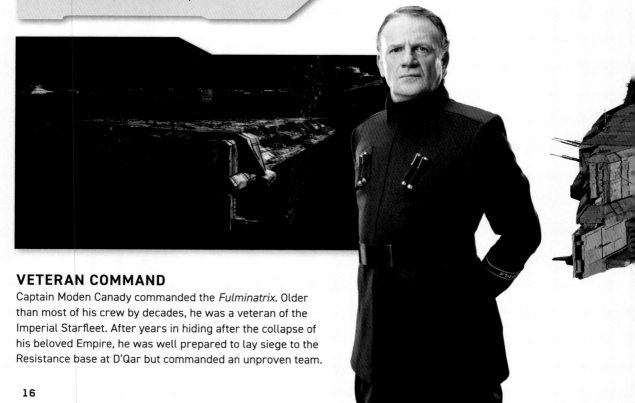

VETERAN COMMAND

Captain Moden Canady commanded the *Fulminatrix*. Older than most of his crew by decades, he was a veteran of the Imperial Starfleet. After years in hiding after the collapse of his beloved Empire, he was well prepared to lay siege to the Resistance base at D'Qar but commanded an unproven team.

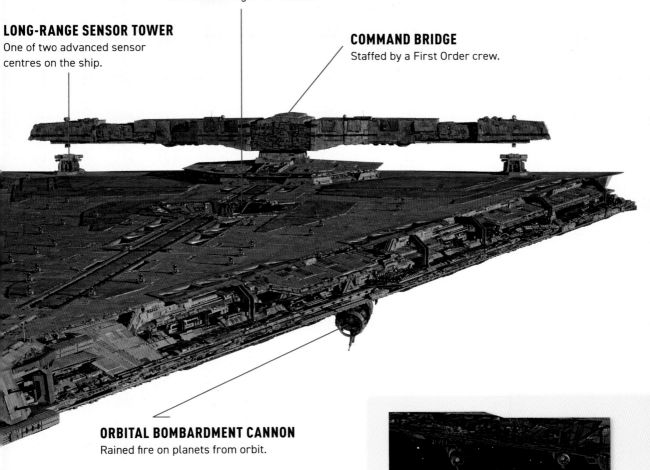

MAIN REACTOR
A direct bomb strike on this reactor led to a devastating chain reaction.

LONG-RANGE SENSOR TOWER
One of two advanced sensor centres on the ship.

COMMAND BRIDGE
Staffed by a First Order crew.

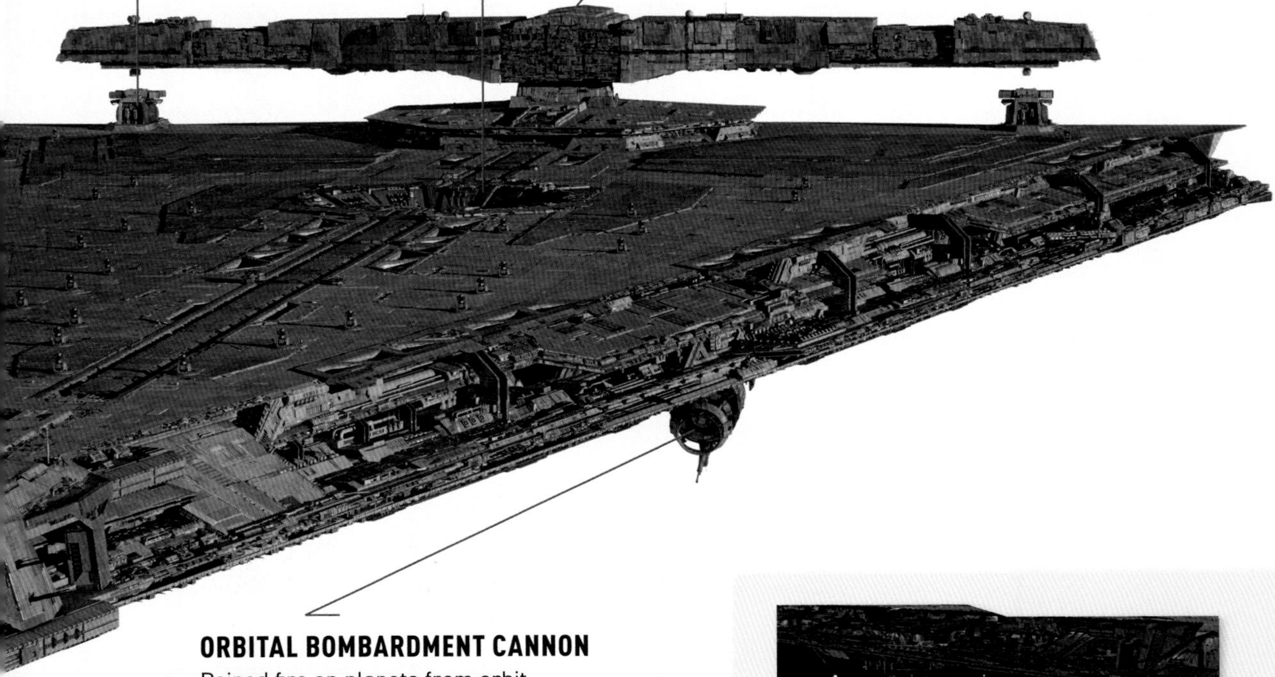

ORBITAL BOMBARDMENT CANNON
Rained fire on planets from orbit.

TRACTOR BEAM PROJECTORS
Captured ships were easy targets for the Dreadnought's cannons.

DOUBLE-BARRELLED
The primary weapons of the *Fulminatrix* were its orbital autocannons. These two artillery guns packed enough firepower to blast their way through planetary shields or lay waste to capital ships.

THE *SUPREMACY*

Supreme Leader Snoke's command ship served as headquarters, home, factory, communications centre and more. This monstrosity was the only *Mega*-class Star Destroyer created and was constructed by the First Order in the furthest reaches of the galaxy. It was destroyed in a courageous act of self-sacrifice by Vice Admiral Holdo of the Resistance.

HEAVY TURBOLASER TOWER
Large cannons fired pinpoint shots at moving targets.

HIDE AND SEEK

Deep within the *Supremacy* lay the tracking room, where the First Order used the latest technology and a massive data warehouse to achieve a strategic feat previously thought impossible: tracking a ship through hyperspace. Ships that attempted to escape by jumping to light speed quickly found that the First Order was right behind them!

TITAN OF INDUSTRY

The *Supremacy* was so large that it could serve as both production facility and shipyard for First Order Star Destroyers. Within the ship were two construction and maintenance facilities staffed with factory workers who worked around the clock. The *Supremacy* housed external docking stations for refuelling and resupplying the fleet of Star Destroyers.

SUPREME LEADER'S THRONE

From his ominous throne room, Snoke commanded the entire First Order and met with Kylo Ren and General Hux. Never far from their master, the Elite Praetorian Guard protected the Supreme Leader from threats.

TECHNICAL SPECIFICATIONS

MANUFACTURER: Kuat-Entralla Engineering

MODEL: *Mega*-class Star Dreadnought

CLASS: Star Dreadnought

LENGTH: 13,239.68 m

WEAPONRY: Thousands of heavy turbolasers, anti-ship missile batteries, heavy ion cannons and tractor beam projectors

CREW: 2,225,000 personnel including officers, stormtroopers, gunners, vehicle engineers, factory workers, technical specialists and communications staff

OVERBRIDGE

Where First Order officers piloted the ship per the Supreme Leader's commands.

SUBLIGHT ENGINE ARRAY

Similar engine technology to the Death Star battle station.

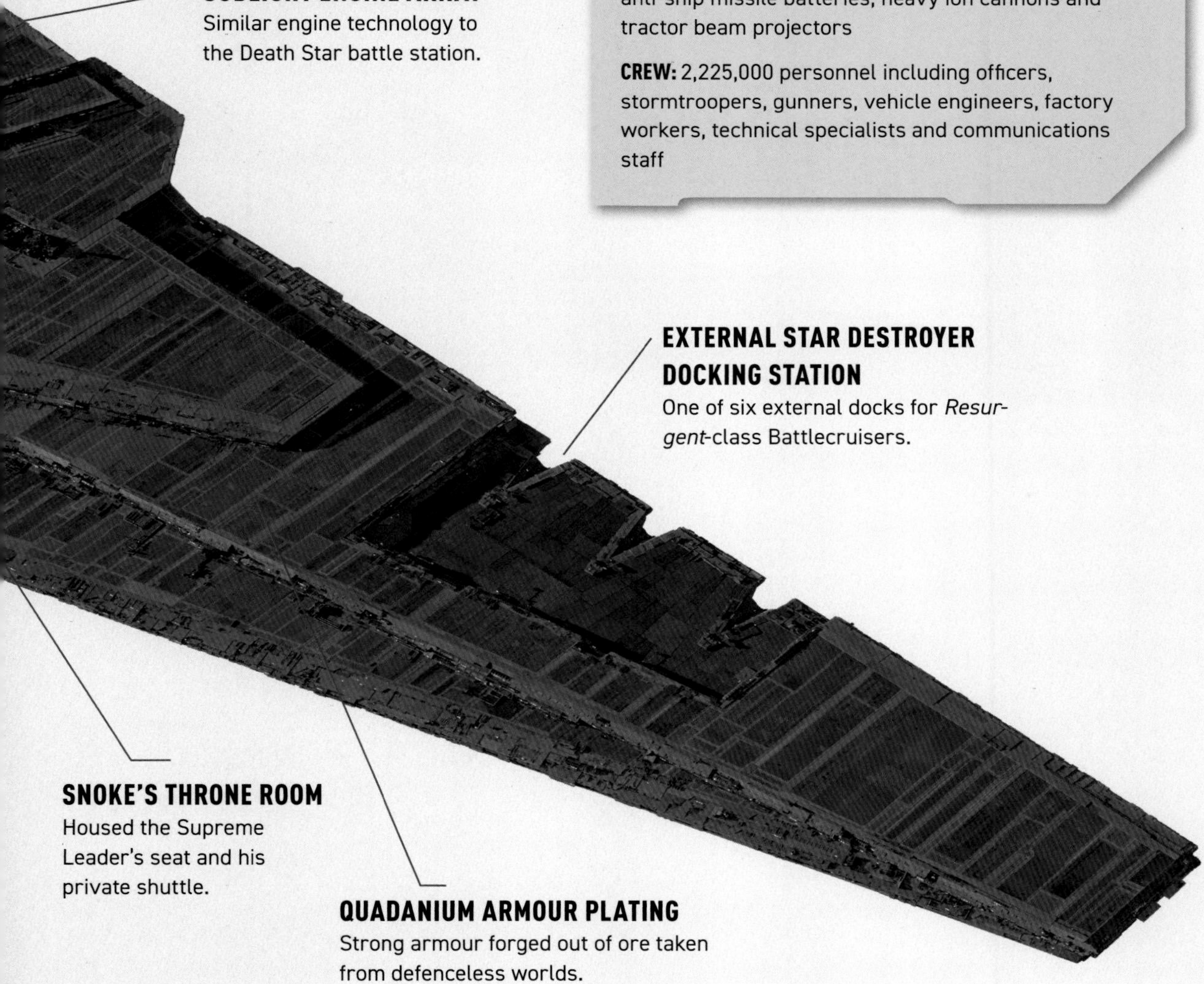

EXTERNAL STAR DESTROYER DOCKING STATION

One of six external docks for *Resurgent*-class Battlecruisers.

SNOKE'S THRONE ROOM

Housed the Supreme Leader's seat and his private shuttle.

QUADANIUM ARMOUR PLATING

Strong armour forged out of ore taken from defenceless worlds.

CLASH OF THE TITANS

Star Destroyers played a pivotal role in some of the galaxy's most crucial battles.

BATTLE OF CORUSCANT

In the closing days of the Clone Wars, Separatist leaders Count Dooku and General Grievous planned a last-ditch effort to kidnap the leader of the Republic, Chancellor Palpatine. Their gambit led to an immense confrontation in the upper atmosphere of the planet with Republic Star Destroyers facing off with Separatist capital ships.

PRINCESS LEIA'S CAPTURE

With the stolen Death Star plans in her possession, Princess Leia fled the battle at Scarif aboard her ship, *Tantive IV*. Darth Vader and his crew aboard the *Devastator* caught up with the Alderaanian vessel above the planet Tatooine. Using turbolasers to knock out the *Tantive IV*'s main reactor, the Imperials easily captured the rebels.

BATTLE OF SCARIF

After discovering that the Empire was constructing a giant battle station with enough power to destroy a planet, the Rebel Alliance attempted to steal the plans for this "Death Star" from the Empire's facility on Scarif. Two Star Destroyers guarding the planet were caught off guard by the rebel fleet, but the arrival of Darth Vader in his *Imperial I*–class Star Destroyer *Devastator* turned the tide in the Empire's favour.

BATTLE OF HOTH

Following the destruction of the Death Star by rebel forces, Darth Vader used probe droids deployed from Star Destroyers across the galaxy to find the rebel base. He eventually tracked the rebels to Hoth, but Admiral Ozzel brought the ship out of hyperspace too close to the system, giving the rebels time to raise their planetary shield and evacuate the base. The rebels had one more surprise for the Imperial fleet: a planetary ion cannon that was able to temporarily disable a Star Destroyer.

BATTLE OF ENDOR

After learning that the Emperor was onboard the second Death Star above the planet Endor, the Rebel Alliance planned a final strike. Little did they know that the intel was part of a trap orchestrated by the Emperor himself. Shortly after the rebel fleet arrived at Endor, the Imperial fleet cornered them. Overconfident in his plan, Palpatine initially ordered his Star Destroyers not to attack the rebels. This attempt to toy with his captives ultimately backfired when the rebels turned the tide and the Death Star was destroyed.

BATTLE OF D'QAR

After the destruction of the New Republic fleet, only General Leia Organa's Resistance was left standing against the might of the First Order. Brave but reckless, Commander Poe Dameron led a direct assault on the Siege Dreadnought *Fulminatrix*. The destruction of the massive ship came at a heavy cost for the Resistance, which lost many of its starfighters and all of its bombers in the battle.

BATTLE ABOVE CRAIT

Out of fuel and unable to evade the First Order, the few remaining ships of the Resistance fleet were easy targets for the *Supremacy*. As the Resistance survivors escaped in shuttles to the nearby planet Crait, Vice Admiral Holdo executed a hyperspace jump at point-blank range, launching a Resistance capital ship into the *Supremacy*. This last-ditch effort destroyed Snoke's flagship, but also the last major vessel in the Resistance fleet.

POE AND FINN'S ESCAPE

Many years after the Galactic Civil War, Resistance pilot Poe Dameron was captured by the First Order and held aboard Kylo Ren's *Finalizer*. Luckily for Poe, a stormtrooper named FN-2187 was ready to desert. Together, Poe and "Finn" – as Poe decided to call his new friend – stole a First Order Special Force TIE fighter but were shot down by the Battlecruiser's point-defense missile system, crash landing on the nearby planet Jakku.

BEHIND THE SCENES

To bring a Star Destroyer to the screen takes teams of artists and model makers working in concert with the storytellers. This is the story of how the colossal craft were created.

CANTWELL'S CONCEPT

Model maker Collin Cantwell was one of the first people hired to work on the original *Star Wars* film. Director George Lucas enlisted Cantwell to create 3D models of the ships he envisioned for his space fantasy. Among the models was a prototype of the Star Destroyer, and even in this prototype, the iconic triangular shape and conning tower were present. The tips of the model included guns, and the tower itself was covered in intricate piping. Though these elements would not carry through to the final filming model, the early and final designs share many similarities.

SIZE MATTERS NOT

When fans first saw *Star Wars* in theaters in 1977, they were blown away by the opening sequence of the Star Destroyer's seemingly never-ending pass overhead. The *Tantive IV* scale model built by the film's special effects team was actually larger than the Star Destroyer model they created. Thanks to careful staging and camera tricks, the Star Destroyer appears much larger in the final shot.

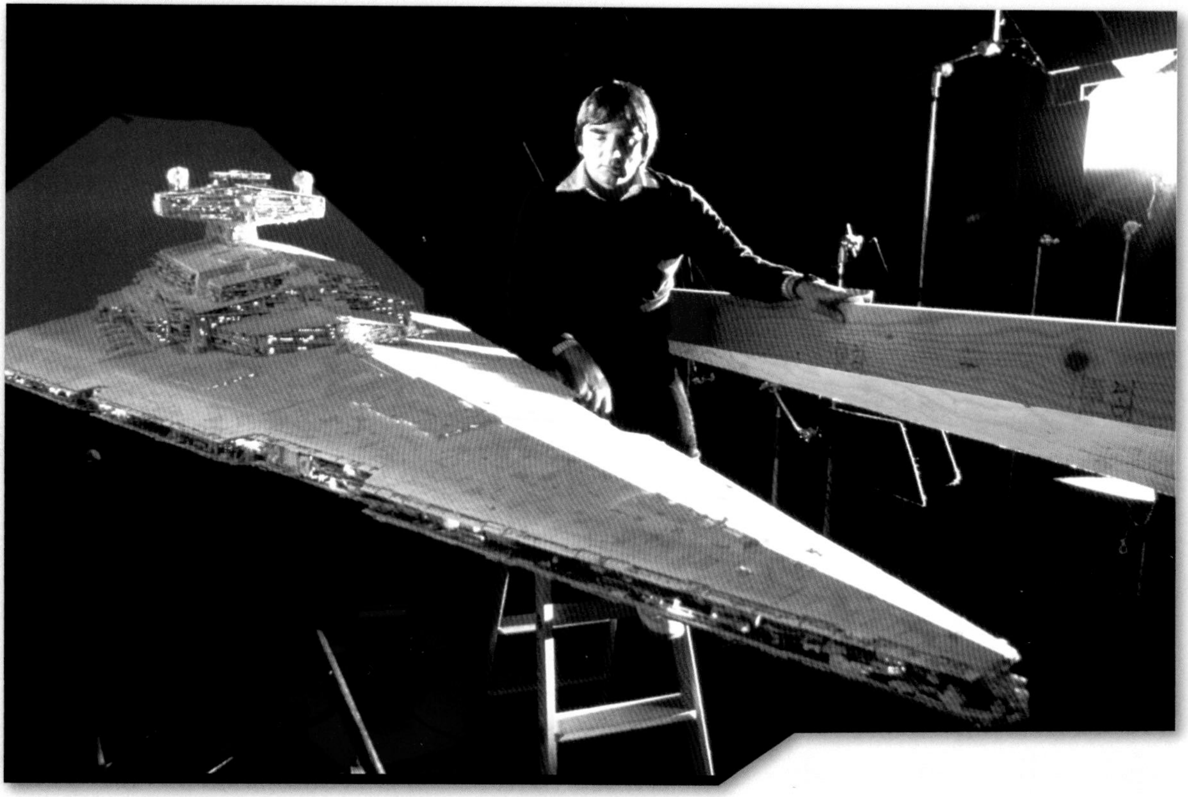

STAR DESTROYER MARK II

Due to the larger role the Star Destroyer would play in *Star Wars: The Empire Strikes Back*, the film's model makers set out to build an all-new model. This time, it would be more than twice the size of the original – 2.4 metres long instead of just 1 metre. Fibre optics and internal halogen bulbs provided hundreds of little lights for the tiny viewports that dot the Star Destroyer's surface.

X MARKS THE SPOT

Sharp-eyed fans will notice a few differences between the model used for *Star Wars* in 1977 and the one in 1980's *The Empire Strikes Back*. The easiest difference to spot is on top of the bridge; the earlier model has a distinctive *X* shape in the centre.

SUPER STAR DESTROYER

Based on a design by Joe Johnston, the Super Star Destroyer model built for *The Empire Strikes Back* was three metres long. To keep the sizable model lightweight, the crew added an aluminum structure similar to those used in airplanes.

EASTER EGG

Hidden among the details of the Star Destroyer is a surprise left by one of the model makers: a small figure of a soldier, likely left over from one of the World War II model kits so frequently used to add detail to ships. Painted blue just like the rest of the *Executor*, the soldier's outstretched arm is only visible up close. The audience would never see it among the tiny features and lights.

PARTING SHOTS

Though the set appears in just one brief scene, a partial Star Destroyer bridge was built for the final sequence in *Star Wars: Revenge of the Sith* (2005). The control pit and some of the bridge window frames were real, but much of the filming set was surrounded by green screen. The green screen would later be digitally replaced with views of space and the under-construction Death Star.

MODERN MARVEL

For *Star Wars: The Force Awakens* (2015), the First Order needed a new Star Destroyer design that was more technologically advanced than the originals. Concept artist James Clyne recalls, "It was fun to work on the Star Destroyer because J. J. [Abrams, director] was heavily involved in the art direction. He threw out all these ideas: 'What if we have negative spaces? What if the tower was asymmetrical?'" Both ideas made it into the final design of the *Finalizer*, Kylo Ren's Star Destroyer.

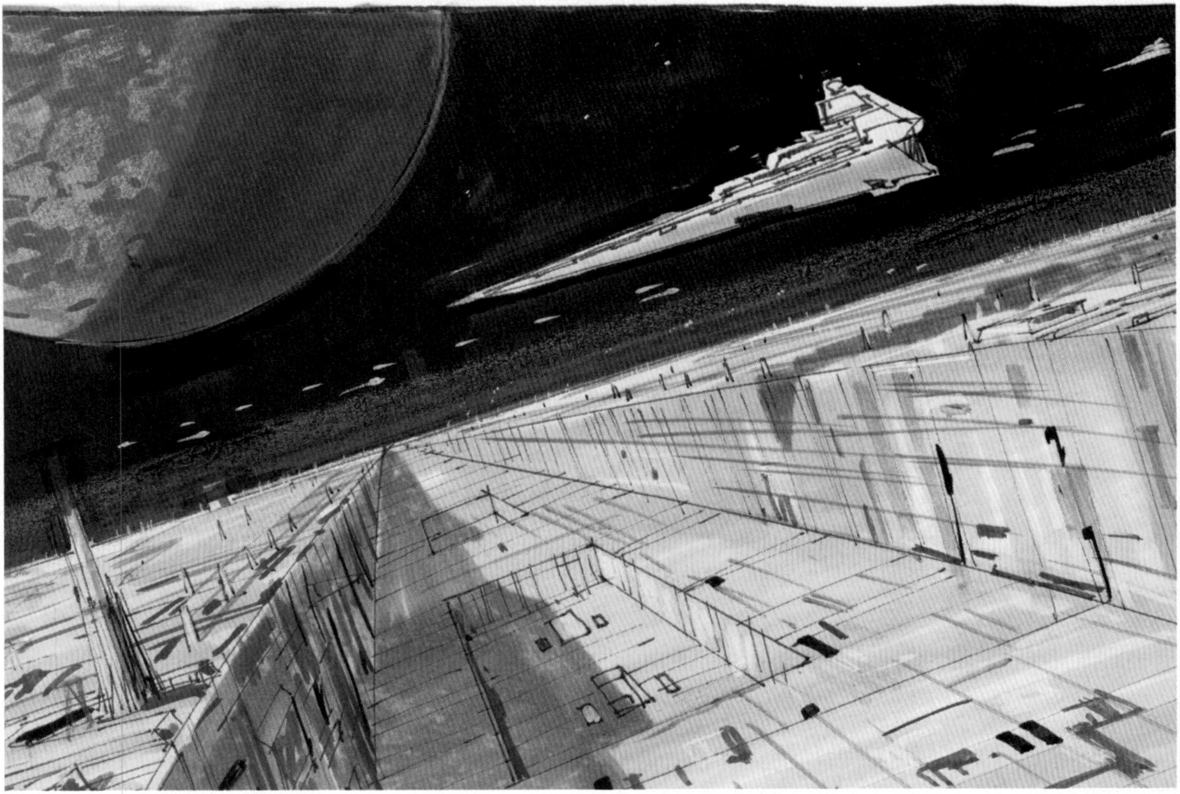

ABOVE: A Star Destroyer flies low over the surface of the second Death Star in this concept piece by Joe Johnston for *Return of the Jedi*.

BELOW: Super Star Destroyer concept art by Joe Johnston for *The Empire Strikes Back*.

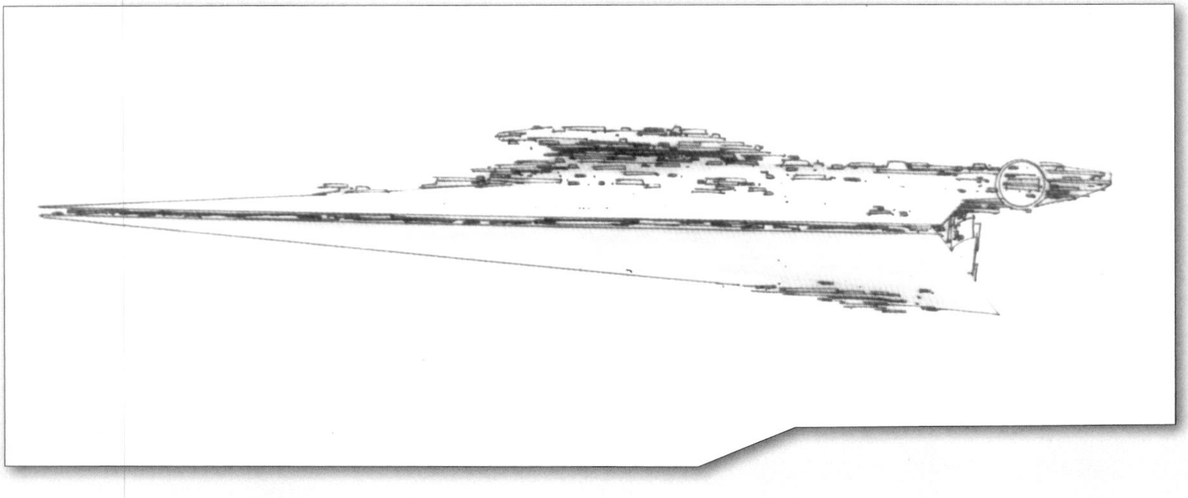

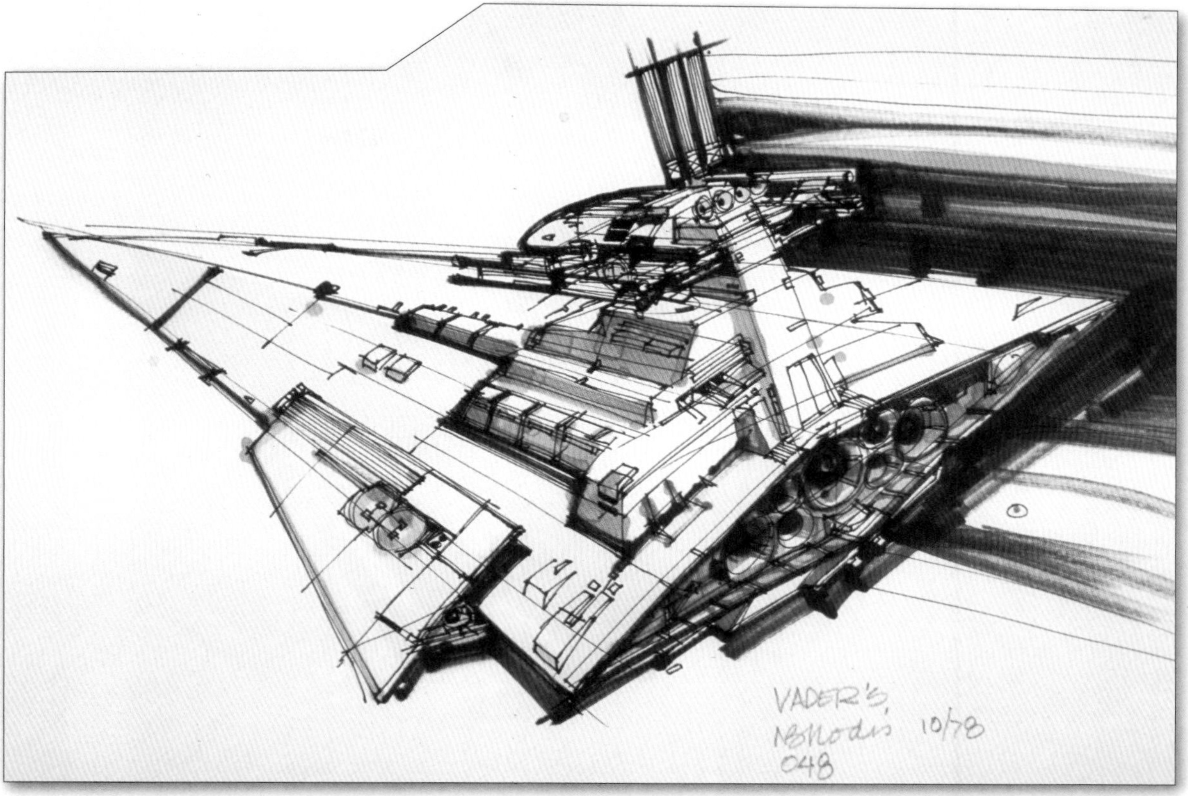

ABOVE: An early Star Destroyer concept sketch by Joe Johnston for *Star Wars* (1977).

BELOW: "Star Destroyer over Jedha Version 2A." Concept art by Andrée Wallin from *Rogue One: A Star Wars Story*.

INTERVIEW WITH PAUL HUSTON

Paul Huston is a veteran of Industrial Light & Magic (ILM). Having served as a model builder on *Star Wars* (1977), he continued to contribute to the saga throughout the original trilogy, including *The Empire Strikes Back* and *Return of the Jedi*. Huston's versatility was put on display throughout his transformative career as he transitioned from model maker to matte artist and later to digital artist. He returned to the saga for the 1997 *Star Wars* special editions and the prequel trilogy of films, working as a digital matte artist. With more than one hundred film credits to his name, he has continued to work at ILM on a variety of films including *The Force Awakens* and *The Last Jedi*.

Your work at ILM goes back to almost the very beginning. As a model maker, did you work on the very first Star Destroyer in *Star Wars*?

Yes, I worked on the metre-long one. I worked on the back end of it. I detailed the area that you see after the ship passes overhead when it's moving away. When you see the engines and the back of the ship, I did a lot of the detailing of that.

What is that detail process like? What methods do you use?

We'd start with a pretty basic shape and then we used model kit parts that we found at a model warehouse, and we bought plastic model kits – battleships, airplanes, and tanks. We had stacks and stacks of those, and we took the kit pieces out because they have so much detail on them and then applied them to the model. We also did a lot of adding small details like piping using wire tubing. For really fine detail, we would scribe lines right into the plastic.

How much time goes into detailing a model like that?

The bottom of the Star Destroyer is approximately 0.3 square metres. There were three people that worked on that for maybe a month or more adding all the little details and the lights. The camera comes really close to

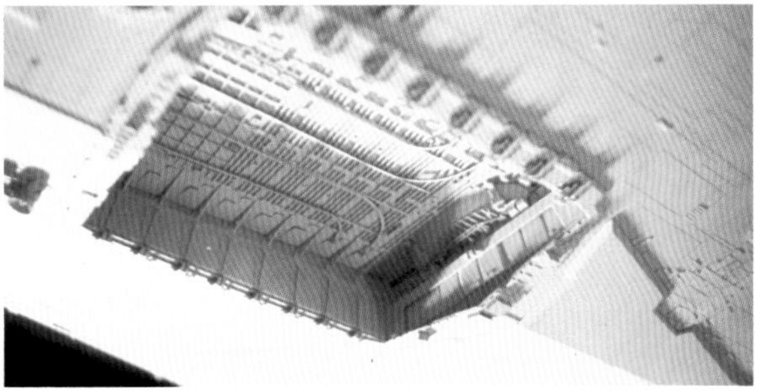

all of that stuff so it really required a lot of very painstaking work to get that to actually hold up.

What was your role in *The Empire Strikes Back* on the new Star Destroyer?

I was the project leader on the 2.4 metre Star Destroyer for *Empire* and I led that effort. I drew up the plans for it based on the one-metre one and I designed the internal structures – the way it was supported, put together, the lighting system, the fiber optics for the lights, the light sources and the cooling. It had to be light enough that it could be supported by the blue screen pylons that we had and also moved fairly easily by a couple of people because there's a lot of switching around between shots. A lot of care was taken in just making sure that the materials were light so the whole thing didn't add up to be a pain to deal with.

We had the one-metre one and then we built almost three other scales based on the action that had to

happen. The smaller one was used for further away, the larger one was used for the medium to close-up, and then there were a couple of sections of really large scale for close-ups like when the *Millennium Falcon* lands on the back of the Star Destroyer conning tower. There was a complete conning tower made for that one that could be at scale with the *Millennium Falcon* model.

Then there was an all-new Star Destroyer, Darth Vader's Super Star Destroyer.

I was the project lead on that one, too. Having the experience of building the 2.4 metre Star Destroyer, there were a lot of ideas to try on Vader's. The lighting needed to be smaller because it's narrower and because the ship itself is supposed to be so much bigger. The size of the lights would be much smaller so that one had fluorescent light bulbs inside and then brass plates with holes – tiny little holes – etched in them for the lights [to shine through].

You've had a long career at ILM that seems to have evolved, much like filmmaking has evolved over the years. How is your experience helping today?

I've made a transition [to working on] 3D modelling, rendering and texturing of environments. I've gone from the physical to the virtual world. The tools have changed a lot but much of the thinking and knowledge required translates really well. It's felt pretty natural. The things that you can do now are just so powerful. It's really been a great evolution of the work.

MAKE IT YOUR OWN

One of the great things about IncrediBuilds™ models is that each one is completely customisable. The untreated, natural wood can be decorated with paints, pencils, pens, beads, sequins – the list goes on and on!

Before you start building and decorating your model, choose a theme and make a plan. You can create a replica of the Star Destroyer, or you can make something completely different. Anything goes! Read through this sample project to get you started and get those creative juices flowing.

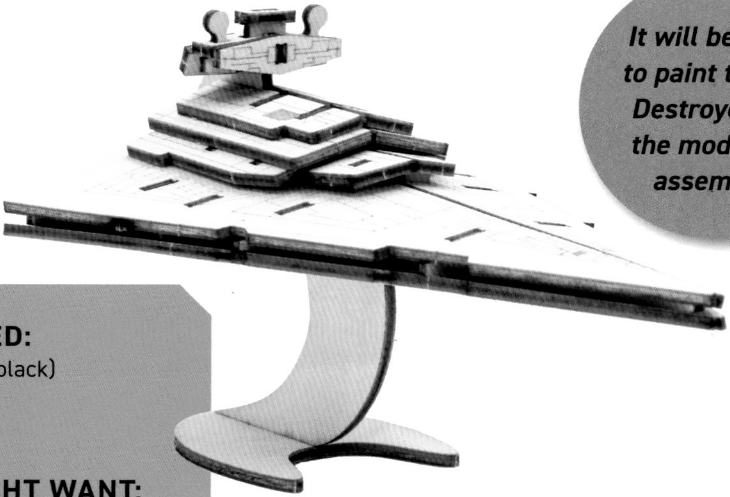

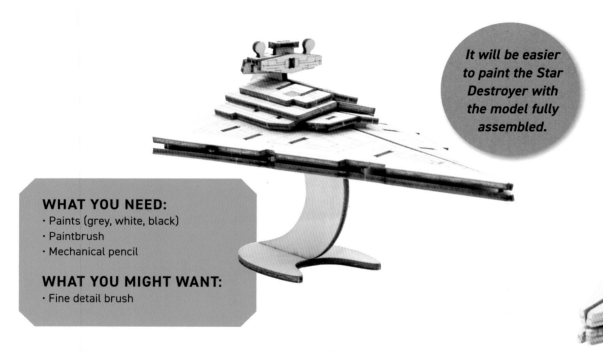

It will be easier to paint the Star Destroyer with the model fully assembled.

WHAT YOU NEED:
- Paints (grey, white, black)
- Paintbrush
- Mechanical pencil

WHAT YOU MIGHT WANT:
- Fine detail brush

1. Start by painting the whole ship a very light grey, almost white.

2. Using a slightly darker paint and a watery brush, paint over the engraved panel seams on the ship's hull. The watery paint should fill the engraved lines and any excess paint can be lightly wiped away with a paper towel.

3. Add even more detail to your ship by drawing on more hull panels with a fine mechanical pencil. Check the reference image – there are thousands of them! The tinier, subtle details you add (even on the edges of the wood), the larger the Star Destroyer will seem... and it should seem immense!

4. Finally, finish off your Star Destroyer by painting the bottom stand black.

GO A STEP FURTHER

To add more detail to your model, use white and dark grey paint to create an extra 3D effect. Consult a reference image in this book to understand which features are raised and which are lower. Use white paint to mimic the raised features. Using the grey paint, darken the areas around the raised features so that the hull around them appears in soft shadow.

INCREDI BUILDS
A Division of Insight Editions
PO Box 3088
San Rafael, CA 94912
www.insighteditions.com
www.incredibuilds.com

Find us on Facebook: www.facebook.com/InsightEditions

Follow us on Twitter: @insighteditions

Library of Congress Cataloging-in-Publication Data available.

ISBN: 978-1-68298-242-6

Publisher: Raoul Goff
Creative Director: Chrissy Kwasnik
Designer: Leah Lauer
Executive Editor: Chris Prince
Editorial Assistant: Hilary VandenBroek
Senior Production Editor: Elaine Ou
Production Director: Lina S Palma
Product Development Manager: Rebekah Piatte
Model Designer: Gina Shi, TeamGreen
Craft Sample: Steve Kongsle

Insight Editions would like to thank Samantha Holland, Michael Siglain, Angela Ontiveros, and Paul Huston.

Manufactured in China

iSeek Ltd, 1A Stairbridge Court, Bolney Grange Business Park, Haywards Heath, RH17 5PA, UK
12 Hatch Street Lower, Dublin, D02 R682, Ireland

Insight Editions, in association with Roots of Peace, will plant two trees for each tree used in the manufacturing of this book. Roots of Peace is an internationally renowned humanitarian organization dedicated to eradicating land mines worldwide and converting war-torn lands into productive farms and wildlife habitats. Roots of Peace will plant two million fruit and nut trees in Afghanistan and provide farmers there with the skills and support necessary for sustainable land use.

ABOUT THE AUTHOR

Cole Horton is an author and games industry professional. He's the coauthor of *Star Wars: Absolutely Everything You Need to Know* and *Star Wars: The Visual Encyclopedia*. Cole lives in San Francisco with his wife. You can find him online at www.ColeHorton.com and on Twitter @ColeHorton.

SOURCES

Dougherty, Kerrie, Curtis Saxton, David West Reynolds, and Ryder Windham. *Star Wars Complete Vehicles*. New York: Dorling Kindersley, 2013.

Fry, Jason. *Star Wars: The Force Awakens, Incredible Cross-Sections*. New York: Dorling Kindersley, 2015.

———. *Star Wars: The Last Jedi, Incredible Cross-Sections*. New York: Dorling Kindersley, 2017.

Hidalgo, Pablo. *Star Wars: The Force Awakens, The Visual Dictionary*. New York: Dorling Kindersley, 2015.

———. *Star Wars: The Last Jedi, The Visual Dictionary*. New York: Dorling Kindersley, 2017.

Peterson, Lorne. *Sculpting a Galaxy: Inside the Star Wars Model Shop*. San Rafael: Insight Editions, 2006.

Rinzler, J. W. *Star Wars Storyboards: The Original Trilogy*. New York: Abrams, 2014.

Szostak, Phil. *The Art of Star Wars: The Force Awakens*. New York: Abrams, 2015.